When Chu sneezed,

bad things happened.

In the morning, Chu went with his mother to the library.

There was old-book-dust
in the air.

"Are you going to sneeze?"
said his mother.

aaah-

aah-

aaaah-

"No," said Chu.

At lunchtime, Chu went with his father to the diner.

There was a lot of pepper
in the air...

"Are you going to sneeze?" asked his father.

AAH-

AAAAH-

AAAAAH-

"No," said Chu.

Later that day, Chu and his
parents went to the circus!

"I will tell you something,"
said Chu.

"I think I am going to sneeze," said Chu.

AAaachoOO

OOOOOO!

"Oops," said Chu.

After the circus,
Chu went to bed.

"Yup," said Chu.
"That was a sneeze all right."

"Goodnight."